Kid Sister

by MARGARET EMBRY

Illustrated by Carol Wilde

SCHOLASTIC BOOK SERVICES

NEW YORK • TORONTO • LONDON • AUCKLAND • SYDNEY

For Pat
and her dear departed Nibbles

This book is sold subject to the condition that it shall not be resold, lent, or
otherwise circulated in any binding or cover other than that in which it is published—unless prior written permission has been obtained from the publisher—
and without a similar condition, including this condition, being imposed on the
subsequent purchaser.

Text copyright 1958 by Holiday House. Illustrations copyright
© 1967 by Scholastic Magazines, Inc. This edition is published
by Scholastic Book Services, a division of Scholastic Magazines,
Inc., by arrangement with Holiday House, Inc.

4th printing .... March 1971

Printed in the U.S.A.

CONTENTS

Homemade Zoo

— 1 —

Zib Pauley hurried through the rain straight to the basement of the church where the Scouts met. She was secretary of Troop 22 for the month of October, and had stayed after school to read once more through the minutes of last week's meeting.

But when she got there the meeting had not yet begun. The girls were still milling about, chattering more excitedly than usual. All Zib could make out was that they were talking about a trip to a zoo.

"Zoo?" she said to Janey Lewis. "What's this about a zoo? There's no zoo here in Brunston, nor any for at least a hundred miles."

"Oh yes there is. Mrs. Thornton just told —
woops, there goes the silence signal!"

Janey wouldn't say another word. She lifted her
right hand with the three fingers pointing toward
the ceiling, and all the other Scouts began to do the
same.

"There, that's a little better," said Mrs. Thornton,
their leader. "Now we can almost hear ourselves
think. All right, Janey, you can take over."

Janey was president for the month, but she was
so new at it she had almost forgotten, and was taking a seat next to Zib instead of up in front at the
table. She rushed up the aisle and picked up the
small wooden hammer.

"Meeting comes to order," she said fiercely. "Is
there any old business, anyone? If not we'll get right
on with — "

"Wait a minute," Zib said, standing and waving
her notebook. "We haven't had the minutes yet."

"Well, O.K. But read them fast, because we've
got something important to do."

Zib read the minutes at breakneck speed, and the
Scouts, who had understood scarcely anything she
said, approved them eagerly as being completely
correct without any additions or other changes.

"Now let's get on to the zoo!" one of the girls broke in.

"O.K., O.K. But I have to tell all of you about it first, don't I?" Janey said. "Well today, kids, we've been invited to visit a homemade zoo. Mrs. Thornton thought, since some of us are beginning to work on our Animal Care Badges, we'd like to see some different kinds of animals and how they live. So she asked Trek Davis if we could visit his collection."

"He keeps them in his garage," one of the Scouts said. "He's got a skunk and just everything. My big brother knows him."

"He's an Explorer Scout," someone else added. "His mother lets him keep some of his animals right in his bedroom."

"O.K., O.K.," Janey said impatiently. "But are we going to sit around all day and just talk about the zoo? Or are we going to visit it?"

"Let's go!" everybody yelled.

"Get in line then," said Mrs. Thornton. "Find a buddy, and get in line. We've got to walk a good half a mile."

Trek was waiting for them beside the open doors of a double garage behind his house. He was a tall blond boy with an easy grin. He went to the same high school as Zib's two big sisters.

"Hi!" He waved. "Come on in!"

Inside the garage the walls were lined on three sides with cages of all sizes and shapes, some of them wooden boxes and some made entirely of wire.

Near the door was a family of brown rabbits. Farther along were two chipmunks, a raccoon, and a coyote pup.

"My uncle sent him to me from Arizona, but he's not tame yet," Trek said.

The little coyote whimpered and moved to the back of his large pen, his hair bristling and his eyes glinting.

From one of the cages Trek pulled out a round bundle of black and white fur. "Now here's my girl friend Millie."

"Oh!" gasped Mrs. Thornton. "It's a skunk!"

The girls squealed and jumped back warily.

But Trek chuckled. "She's been deodorized, don't worry."

"Ah!" said Mrs. Thornton. She stroked the thick black hair. "Isn't she a sweet baby!"

"Do you want to hold her?" Trek said.

Mrs. Thornton reached out her arms and the baby skunk cuddled down against her shoulder. All of the girls clamored for turns while Millie was passed lovingly from one to the other.

Trek let them feed her bits of a chocolate bar that he had in his pocket. She took the chunks in her clever black hands and sat up like a monkey to eat.

Zib felt a rush of delight. How she'd like to have a pet like Millie! But a skunk? She could imagine what Mom would say. And Ruth and Karen would be horrified at the very thought.

"Did you see these baby owls, girls?" Mrs. Thornton asked. "They're not even in a cage."

"I've only had these two fellows a few days," Trek explained. "I got them in a barn out in the country. I've got to be building a cage for them or they'll fly away."

The two little owls sat solemnly on a tree branch fastened between two cages. Trek lifted one of them off. He held his finger close to the owl's eyes, then moved his hand slowly around behind.

"Look how he can turn his head."

The round, fuzzy head followed Trek's finger completely around.

"Golly," said Janey. "I wish *I* could do that!"

"It would save time if you wanted to see if the person in back of you is correcting your spelling paper right," said Zib thoughtfully.

"Be mighty handy," agreed Trek. "I can think of dozens of uses for a good swivel neck. Well, that's about all the creatures I have here in the garage. Let me put Millie back in her cage."

He took the little skunk from Zib's arms. How she hated to give her up! A whole minute afterward Zib could still feel the soft warmth of the baby animal.

Millie leaned against the door of her cage and looked out disappointedly, making sad mewing sounds like a kitten.

"I've got some more animals upstairs in my room, if you'd like to see them," Trek said.

The Scouts did not wait to be asked twice. They trooped excitedly after him, through the kitchen where his mother was starting supper, and up the hall stairs to his room.

It did not look like a bedroom at all except for the bed. There were tanks of tropical fish on the window sill and floor, and a metal box on the dresser that held a sleeping alligator.

"Jiminy! Doesn't your mother care?" Zib asked.

"Care? Why should she?" Trek shrugged. "As long as I look after them. But she won't even come inside my room. She leaves my clean shirts hanging out on the banister. I think she's afraid of the alligator. Or maybe it's my friend Bobo she doesn't like."

From under the bed he pulled a flat, oblong box with a screen at one end. He opened the top and reached in, pulling out an enormous snake. The girls yelped and jumped back.

"Oh, he won't hurt you," Trek said. "He's a bull snake. He's really very friendly." The snake wrapped his long gray self affectionately around Trek's arm.

"Go ahead, touch him. Really, he won't hurt you."

But even Mrs. Thornton shook her head.

Zib waited a minute, then put her finger out carefully and stroked the snake's back. She was surprised to find how dry he felt. "I thought he'd be kind of slimy."

"No, snakes never are unless they are living in wet, slimy places," Trek said. "Their bodies are

pretty much the same temperature as their sur-
roundings, and this fellow living under my bed
here is nice and warm. Want to hold him?"

And before Zib could say no, he had handed her
the snake. She tried to grasp Bobo around the middle, but he slid easily around her arms and draped
himself quite at home around her shoulders.

Trek grinned. "He likes you."

Zibby wasn't at all sure that she completely returned his affections, but she pretended. She petted
his long back, and she could feel his muscles
tighten.

All of the other Scouts were very impressed.
Janey got up a little more courage and put out her
hand toward Bobo. His swift tongue darted out at
her, and he hissed. She jumped back with a squeal.

"Don't be afraid," Trek told her. "He's not going
to bite. That's his way of finding out about you. He
hears and smells with his tongue."

"Why, I always thought that was his stinger!"
Zib said before she thought. And all the girls
laughed. Zib was mortified that she was so igno-
rant, but Mrs. Thornton said that was exactly what
she too used to think.

"It still makes me shiver when a snake flips out
his tongue at me like that."

"He doesn't have a stinger at all," Trek explained. "He has some very ordinary teeth." Trek squeezed Bobo's mouth open and showed them the rows of tiny needle-sharp teeth. "He's a nonpoisonous snake, so he doesn't have fangs like a rattler."

"Doesn't he ever bite you?" asked one of the girls.

"Hardly ever, if I handle him gently. He's really quite fond of me. And his bite is just like a needle prick. It doesn't hurt very much."

"What does he eat?" Zib wanted to know.

"Oh, mice or frogs, or young rats. He likes to have all his food alive. That reminds me, here's something else I'll bet you'd like to see."

Trek laid Bobo carefully back in his box and pushed him under the bed. Then he reached further under for a sturdy metal cage. He unhooked the door and made a sharp clucking noise with his tongue. In the middle of the cage was a heap of shredded paper which began to wobble. Out from the top of it, like a small volcano erupting, came a black nose, followed immediately by a white body, with an amazing number of pink grublike creatures clinging to its sides.

"Why, it's a mother rat!" Mrs. Thornton said,

leaning over the cage. "And look at all her babies!"

"This is Mamie," Trek said proudly. "And her family. All nine of them. They were born last Wednesday."

"They're not even a week old yet," Janey said, crowding in to see. "Aren't they funny!"

"She doesn't look like an ordinary white rat," Mrs. Thornton said. "Look at her black face and head."

"She's a hooded rat," Trek said. "You don't often see one as perfectly marked as this one. The black and white variations are getting more common among laboratory strains, but the hooded ones are still quite a special breed. See, even her eyes and ears are black."

Mamie carelessly shook her hungry offspring loose, and came over to the open cage door to sniff and see if there was anything for her to eat. One of the infants scrambled after her and tumbled out onto the floor.

Quickly Zib scooped it up in her hand. "Hey, you, where do you think you're going?"

The girls all crowded around to see what she had.

"Why, the poor little thing hasn't got its eyes open yet," Janey said.

"You little dope," Zib said tenderly, "you might have got stepped on."

"But maybe the mother doesn't want anybody to handle her babies," said Mrs. Thornton glancing toward Trek questioningly.

He was busy giving Mamie some bits of oatmeal cookies out of his pocket. "That's right," he said. "I'm afraid she'll kill that little one if we put it back now. I make it a rule never to handle the young animals until they at least have their eyes open. Mother rodents, such as rats, hamsters, and rabbits, are awfully particular about human smell on their babies."

"Oh!" Zib said. "I didn't even think. I didn't want it to get stepped on."

"Can we wash it off?" Janey asked.

Trek shook his head. "No, it would never work. She'd still know you had handled it."

Trek took the tiny infant from Zib. "It's a stubborn little guy, look," and he flipped it over with his thumb onto his palm. The baby immediately twisted and turned until it was back onto its little toothpick legs. It stood unsteadily and then wobbled over to the edge of Trek's hand and stopped short.

"Look, it knows already there's danger," Zib said. "It won't go any further."

"Look at its whiskers!" Janey said. "They look like silver hairs, they're so tiny."

"She looks as though she's going to be hooded like her mother. See," said Trek. "There's just a faint smoky tinge to the hair across her shoulders."

The Scouts all crowded around to see.

"I can't see that she's got any hair on her at all," Janey said. "She looks mighty bare to me."

"She is pretty bare, all right," said Trek, "but when I hold her right in the light you can see the dark fuzz on her."

"I see it! I see it!" Zib said, jumping. Then she asked, "What are you going to do with her?"

"Oh, I guess I might as well give her to Bobo. It would make a nice treat for his supper."

"Oh no!" cried the Scouts.

"Why not?" Trek said. "She'll just get killed if I try to put her back in the nest, and she'll starve to death without her mother."

"Give her to me!" Zib said suddenly, before she knew what she was doing.

"What would you do with her?" Trek frowned.

"Feed her warm milk with a doll's bottle," Zib

mused. "And I'd keep her safe and warm."

Trek still looked at her sternly.

"She'd live, I know she would. Let me try, please, Trek!"

"You'd have to feed her every hour or so. And that means all night too. Do you think it's worth it?"

"Oh yes," Zib answered eagerly. "I can do it. I know I can. And I don't have a pet. Any kind of pet."

"Do you think she could, Trek?" Mrs. Thornton asked.

"Oh, I think so. If she keeps working at it. I raised a whole litter of tiny rabbits once after their mother had died. You don't feed them ordinary milk. You have to make a sort of formula. You put a little bit of water with it, and a pinch of sugar. Or corn syrup would be better. And later on you give it some cod-liver oil. But not too much, or you'll have a sick rat."

Zib was listening carefully, trying to remember it all.

"Here, I'll write it down for you, so you'll be sure and do it right." Trek hunted up a pencil and a scrap of paper from his cluttered desk.

Zib felt in her pockets for a piece of Kleenex to wrap her new pet in, but she had only a crumpled one. Mrs. Thornton got a fresh, neatly folded tissue out of her purse, and they carefully swathed it around the infant.

"Gee, you're lucky," Janey said, as they walked downstairs and outside. "I wish I had thought of asking for it!"

Zib put the piece of paper with the formula written on it carefully into the same pocket with the tiny pet. She closed her fingers over the precious tissue, to help keep the baby warm and safe until she got home.

She ran the five blocks home through the chilly dusk, chanting to herself, "You've got to live. You've got to live. You've got to live till I get home."

She cut down the back alley, because it was quicker than going around, and skipped up the back porch steps. Just as she opened the door, she whispered, "I know what I'll name you: Rosemary! Because you are tiny and sweet and bright pink."

Four Thirty A.M.

— 2 —

WHEN ZIB OPENED THE KITCHEN DOOR, there was the good warm smell of supper cooking and the sound of Karen practicing in the living room. Zib's mother was just dishing up the potatoes, and turned around when she heard Zib come in. There were two worry lines between her eyes.

"Zibby! Where have you been?"

"At Scouts, Mom. It's Tuesday, remember?"

"Oh, that's right," Mrs. Pauley said a little easier. "But it's so late. Why do you always have to stay until after dark? I needed you to run to the store for me. But it's closed now."

Zib's older sister, Ruth, came in from the dining room. "You'll have to help with the dishes, punk, because I helped with supper. Besides, I've got a ton of homework. What on earth were you doing at Scouts for two whole hours?"

"I came home as fast as I could," Zib said. "But our troop went over to Trek Davis' to see his animals. And look!" Zib pulled the Kleenex out of her pocket and carefully unfolded it. The little creature was still alive, and lay shivering on her hand.

"Oooh!" gasped Mrs. Pauley. "What is it? A mouse?"

Ruth leaned over her shoulder. "Where did you get it? What a nasty naked little thing it is!"

"It's not nasty," Zib said angrily, pulling the paper tissue up warmer around the tiny beast. "Trek gave it to me. It's a very special kind of hooded rat. And I'm going to keep it and raise it."

"Well, you should have left it with its mother. It's not even finished yet," Ruth said unsympathetically.

"What's not finished yet? Supper?" Mr. Pauley came in from the living room with the newspaper in his hand. "I've got a Lodge meeting tonight, and it's getting pretty late."

"Supper's ready. I'm just putting it on the table," Mrs. Pauley said. "Take your rat out of the kitchen, Zibby. I don't want it around the food."

"But where can I put it, Mom? I'll need a box."

"Rat? What rat?" her father asked.

"Zibby's rat," Ruth pointed. "Right there in her hand. It's not even big enough to have its eyes open yet."

"Let me see it," Mr. Pauley demanded. "Mmh — it's only a suckling." He looked a bit interested for a moment, then turned away. "Rats are nothing but pests, Zib. They don't make good pets."

"This one will, Daddy, honest. It's a very special kind of rat. Look, you can see already where she's going to be hooded."

Mr. Pauley again looked close. "Can't see a thing but pink fuzz."

Mrs. Pauley shook her head firmly. "We don't have room in the house for a pet, Zibby. You know that. And I especially can't stand the thought of a rat!"

Karen stuck her head in the hall door. "When are we going to eat?"

Nobody had noticed that she had finished her practicing.

She glanced scornfully at Zib's hand. "What's that thing supposed to be?"

"It's a purebred hooded rat," Zib answered, "and you can just leave it alone."

"Take the thing outside, Zibby," Mrs. Pauley said again. "I can't have it here in the kitchen."

"But, Mom, it will freeze outside. Can't I put it in a box and keep it in my room?"

Mrs. Pauley set the dish of potatoes down with a sigh, opened the cupboard, and reached in for a matchbox. She dumped the matches into an empty pickle jar and handed the box to Zib.

"You'll find some more Kleenex in the linen closet upstairs. It's shivering. You'd better see that it's good and warm. What are you going to feed it?"

Zib was already darting for the stairs, yelling back her thanks. "I've got the formula all written down. Can I get an old medicine dropper out of the bathroom?"

The rest of the family sat down to supper while Zib, back again in the kitchen, fussed over her little pet. Finally her mother came out and helped her measure the corn syrup. And then all the others came after her, letting the food on the table get cold while they watched the feeding process.

Mrs. Pauley had to press the tight little mouth open so that Zib could drop in the milk, but once the baby got the taste, she began to swallow eagerly, and clung to the dropper with her tiny front paws.

"Why she's trying to suckle," Mrs. Pauley said.

"Of course she's trying, Mom," Zib said quickly. "Isn't that cute? What a determined little thing she is!"

Her mother looked closely.

"Look at her little toenails," Zib said.

"It is amazing how perfect such a tiny creature can be," Mrs. Pauley observed. "Even though her eyes aren't open and she doesn't have much hair."

"You sound as interested as if it were your own baby, Mom," Ruth teased.

Mrs. Pauley blushed. "Well, there is something about a helpless little creature that makes me feel motherly. Even if it's only a rat."

"She isn't any old rat," Zib said patiently. "I keep telling you she's a very special —"

"We know, we know, punk," Ruth moaned. "She's all decked out like little Red Riding Hood, except you can't see it yet. For all you know it'll be bright red, and then we can name her Little Red —"

"She's already named, so there! I'm going to call her Rosemary."

"Rosemary?" Karen shouted. "What a name for a rat!"

"What's the matter with Rosemary?" Zib asked defiantly.

"It's a crazy name for a rat, that's what," Karen shot back.

"Why don't you name her Nibbles or Scrambles or Whitey?" Mr. Pauley suggested.

"Or Hoodie?" Ruth snickered.

"Rosemary's a pretty girl's name, dear," Mrs. Pauley said gently. "Don't waste it on a rat."

"It won't be wasted," Zib answered. "It's Miss Barnes's name, and she would be proud to have me name my first pet after her. She even looks a little like Miss Barnes."

"Oh no!" wailed Ruth. Karen smacked her hand against her forehead in despair. Miss Barnes was Zib's fifth-grade teacher. She was small and quick, and had a rosy freckled face, but no one but a dope like Zib would say she looked like a rat!

"Well, the rat probably won't live until morning anyway," Mr. Pauley reasoned. "So Miss Barnes won't have to be concerned about her namesake."

"Oh Daddy!" Zib pleaded. "She *will* live. She's got to live. I'm going to stay awake all night and feed her. All of you are getting fond of her. You know you are!"

But not one of them would admit it. Karen and Ruth suddenly remembered they had let their suppers get cold. Mrs. Pauley began bustling about, reheating potatoes and meat. She did not mention the rat any more, but she did not make Zib take it out of the kitchen.

Zib tried her best to stay awake all night. She brought a blanket down to the dining room and curled up on the old studio couch there so she would be near the kitchen, where she could warm Rosemary's formula.

She fed the baby rat every hour until midnight, and then fell sound asleep.

Dreaming about Bobo the bull snake starving to death because there was nothing to feed him, she awoke with a sick, guilty start, realizing she'd over-slept.

There was a light on in the kitchen, and someone was working at the stove. Zib tumbled off the couch and came into the light, squinting her eyes at its

brightness. Daddy was standing at the stove, warming the medicine bottle of Rosemary's formula in a small pan of water.

"How is she?" Zib asked. "I guess I must have slept too long. What time is it?"

"Four thirty a.m. The varmint's still kicking and hunting for food. When did you feed her last?"

Zib rubbed her eyes and yawned and tried to remember. It all seemed like a misty dream now. She couldn't remember how many times she'd gotten up or when, but it was a lot.

"Well, anyway, it looks as though she might make it," Daddy said cheerfully, squirting a drop of milk onto his arm to test it. "She looks a lot livelier than she did last night."

Zib picked up Rosemary and was surprised to feel how hard the tiny legs could push in a struggle to wriggle free. She cuddled the baby in the palm of her hand, tipping her up so Daddy could put the medicine dropper in the seeking little mouth.

"Aren't you sort of glad, Daddy, that I've found a pet?"

He stretched and yawned, "I only know that I'm dead on my feet. My baby-feeding nights should have been over a good ten years ago, but it looks as though they are beginning again."

Zib chuckled, "At least we won't have to burp her. And she won't yell with the colic the way you said I did."

"Oh, you weren't so bad," he said, giving her hair an affectionate tousle. "I used to sort of enjoy walking the floor with you. That's how we first got acquainted."

Zib looked around the bright kitchen. It had never looked so warm and cozy before. She felt happy enough to burst. "Isn't it fun!" she said. "Just to be the only ones in the whole family awake."

Starve Together

— 3 —

AFTER ROSEMARY HAD LIVED in the large match-box for a week, she learned to climb out; so Zib moved her to an empty shoebox. Rosemary then slept upstairs under her mistress' bed and soon learned to take her milk out of a doll's bottle, which was propped up for her so that she could drink whenever she was hungry. Zib now could sleep through the night, and the arrangement worked well also during the day while she was at school.

One afternoon Trek came by on his bicycle on his way home from delivering papers. "I just wondered how you and the rat pup were making out?" he said.

Zib ran upstairs to get Rosemary.

Trek held Rosemary in his hand and said, "She's doing wonderfully well. I don't think her own mother could have done better. You might start on Pablum now and some soft bread and milk."

Karen heard them talking on the front porch, so she opened the door and said, "Well, my goodness, Zibby, why don't you ask Trek to come into the house?"

Zib did not know what to say. She hadn't even thought that he might like to come in and sit down. But Trek said he was in pretty much of a hurry to get home. He'd stop by again and see how things were going.

"Come over any time, Zib," he said, slowly pedaling away. "I'll lend you a book I have about mammals."

Karen followed Zib back upstairs and into her bedroom, while she put Rosemary away in her box. "For lop's sake, Zib, that's no way to treat a boy, keeping him standing there talking about an old rat."

"Well, golly!" Zib said hotly. "That's the only reason he came. He likes rats and snakes. He sure didn't come to see you."

"I didn't say he did. But at least you might — Oh, you're too young. You wouldn't understand!" Karen flounced out and stomped into her own room.

The next afternoon after school Zib and Rosemary paid Trek a return visit. Rosemary rode in Zib's coat pocket again, but she made a sizable lump in it now. Zib was anxious to see how well Rosemary compared with her brothers and sisters.

Trek put the eight little rats out on his desk. They snuffled suspiciously at their sister, and crowded against her threateningly. Rosemary backed away in fear, and Zib scooped her up quickly, a bit afraid that they might hurt her.

"She's just as big and healthy as they are," Trek said. "But she's quite outnumbered."

"What are you going to do with all of them?" Zib asked. "They're almost big enough to leave their mother, aren't they?"

"Sure, in another week they'll be eating any- and everything. I've promised two of the kids in my Scout troop a couple of them, and my biology teacher wants the rest. He uses them in experiments."

"Oh," said Zib relieved, "I thought you were going to feed them to your snake."

"Bobo? Oh, he'd like that all right, but I get sort

of attached to the little scamps when they're this big. They're beginning to look like respectable rats at last."

"What does Bobo get to eat, then?"

"Oh, most of the time he only gets hamburger. And he hates it, so he sulks and won't eat for several days. Then, if I feel sorry enough for him, I catch him some frogs or field mice."

"Field mice!" said Zib, thinking of the soft little brown frightened creatures.

"Oh, I don't mind getting rid of a few field mice. They don't seem to have nearly as much personality as rats. And they can't compare when it comes to intelligence. Besides, they always smell so much like mice. Rats are nearly odorless, you've probably noticed."

"Yes, I have," Zib agreed. "Even Ruth and Karen don't complain about that."

Trek had tucked Mamie's litter back in the cage with her, and they scrambled toward her eagerly. "Enjoy your mom while you can, kids; you'll be off in the cold cruel world next week."

He pushed the cage back under the bed and pulled out Bobo's flat box. "Hi there, feller," he said affectionately, "do you want to come out?"

Zib hoped he wasn't going to ask her if she'd like

to hold the snake, and he didn't. He didn't bother to ask her at all. Instead, he just handed her Bobo and said, "Here, you mind him while I feed the fish and the alligator."

The big snake writhed up her arms and across her shoulders again. This time it was much easier. "You're not really such a bad guy, after all," Zib whispered to him. And out loud to Trek, she said, "You know, I'd like to have a pet like him. But golly! Wouldn't Ruth and Karen have a fit!"

Trek chuckled in sympathy. "When you've had enough of him, just put him back in his box. Be sure the lid is fastened securely, because he is a rascal for getting out."

Bobo acted as though he hated to leave Zib, and she had to peel him off her arm. "Get in there now," she told him. "I can't spend all my time with you!"

Trek was looking at his wrist watch. "Woops, it's later than I thought, Zib. I've got to get started on my paper route. I'll get that book for you. Take your time about bringing it back. And keep me posted on how Rosemary is doing. You're doing a fine job."

In another two weeks Rosemary was eating bread

besides her Pablum, and bits of vegetables and meat. She was covered with a soft white coat topped by the jet-black hood extending over her head and shoulders.

She had a row of fine sharp teeth, with the two side top ones, much longer than the rest, jutting out over her lower jaw. Her eyes were like two dark shiny marbles, sometimes glinting blue when she was frightened.

She walked with an uncertain waddle, lifting her head to sniff and peer about like a nearsighted old lady. Zib wondered how she would look in a tiny pair of glasses. But Rosemary seemed quite able to depend on her alert little ears and keen sense of smell. She very rarely tumbled off a chair or bed now, but sniffed cautiously when she came to the edge, then backed away.

She made a nest out of the tissues Zib gave her, and curled up tightly in it and slept all day until Zib came home from school and called her to come out. First her small black nose would poke up, with the whiskers wriggling inquisitively. As soon as she made sure it was Zib, she tumbled forth eagerly and asked to be taken out of her box.

While Zib lay on her stomach on the bed doing

her homework, Rosemary scuttled back and forth among the papers, playing hide-and-seek. It was hard to concentrate on arithmetic while watching her.

Rosemary often came down to supper concealed in Zib's pocket, and was fed scraps from the table. This went on until Ruth caught sight of the rat's eager nose and reported it to the rest of the family.

"Elizabeth!" Mrs. Pauley exclaimed, "you take her right back upstairs! I won't have a rat in the dining room."

"But, Mom, you didn't mind her at first when she was tiny. You helped me feed her in the kitchen."

"That was before she looked so much like a rat," Ruth said. "But there's no mistaking what she is now."

"I think she's pretty," Zib said rubbing her cheek against Rosemary's sleek head.

Mr. Pauley frowned. "She's still just a rat."

"No, she isn't, Daddy. She's not a wild rat, but a very special breed, like fancy breeds of dogs in a high-class dog show."

"Look at her stringy tail," Karen said.

Zib looked at her tail. "What's wrong with it? It's a very efficient tail. Almost as useful as another

hand or foot. Look how she hangs on with it. Look, Mom, no claws!" Zib showed them how Rosemary could balance herself on her mistress' arm, clinging only by her long powerful tail. "Why, if you had a tail like that, just think what you could do, Mom!"

"I'm glad I don't have a tail like that!" was the answer. "Take her upstairs, Zibby, and don't bring her down again."

"Not even to play with her? If I promise not to let her into the kitchen or dining room?"

Mrs. Pauley looked at Mr. Pauley, and then said, "Well, you may take her into the hall, but only on your way outside. You may play with her on the back porch."

"Not in the living room?" Zib asked, just testing.

"No!" her mother and Ruth said together.

Karen added, "She'll bother me while I practice."

"She doesn't bother anyone," Zib said. "But she has very sensitive ears, and it certainly bothers her when you hit all those sour notes!"

Karen jumped out of her chair to whack Zib, but Zib was too quick for her, and beat her to the hall door.

Then Zib remembered one more question: "Can I please take her into the bathroom sometimes, Mother?"

Mrs. Pauley looked up from her plate. "Heavens, no! Why should she need to be in the bathroom?"

"Because while I'm cleaning out her box, I have to put her in some safe place where she won't get loose. So I let her run around in the bathtub. Without any water in it, of course. She pretends she's climbing the Alps."

Ruth shrieked. "In the bathtub! I'm not going to bathe in there again. After that dirty little thing has been messing in it."

"She's not dirty!" Zib yelled. "She's a lot cleaner than you are. She washes herself all over every time after humans have handled her."

"Oh, for lop's sake!" said Karen, getting up angrily. "I'm not going to stay here if that child is going to be allowed to stand here with that rat. She's spoiled my whole supper!"

Mr. Pauley picked up his fork. "Zib, take that animal out of here! Karen, sit down and eat your supper."

Zib took Rosemary and stamped all the way up the stairs. She banged the door to her room and heard them shout at her, but she paid no attention.

She lay on her bed and thought harsh things about her whole family, and whispered them to Rosemary, who ran back and forth across the bedspread, hunting for some arithmetic papers to chew on.

Finished with her exploring, Rosemary clambered up Zib's chest, marched across her shirt front, and settled down in her favorite spot under Zib's collar. Her claws tickled, and Zib had to giggle in spite of her mood. Rosemary snuffled and squeaked happily in her ear.

"We'll just stay up here and starve together, Rosie. We'll never go downstairs. They'll be sorry!"

But a little later Zib remembered that there had been lemon pie for dessert, so she tiptoed down to the kitchen. Dinner was long over, and the rest of the family were in the living room, watching television. At least she had got out of helping with the dishes.

Her half-eaten plate of supper was sitting on top of the potato kettle, covered over with a pie tin, and was still warm. Zib took it, and found her piece of pie in the refrigerator. She poured herself a fresh glass of milk. And then, balancing it all very carefully, she went back upstairs quietly to share it with her pet.

The bits of meatloaf and vegetables Rosemary carried off to store thriftily in her nest, but the spoonful of pie Zib offered her, she seized greedily in her two front paws, sitting up like a hungry chipmunk and gobbling it noisily — the lemon filling, meringue, and all.

Bathroom Battle

— 4 —

THE NEXT WEEK ROSEMARY DISAPPEARED. Zib woke as usual one morning, not suspecting anything was wrong. She felt under her bed for the shoebox, just as she always did. The box was there, and the soft white tissue nest, but no hopeful little black nose poked itself out when she called.

She stirred the pieces of Kleenex, then picked them up one by one and shook them out. A small crust of bread, a bit of cabbage, and a dried stringbean tumbled out. But no Rosemary.

She just couldn't be gone! Zib got down on her hands and knees, and looked under the bed. There were several rolls of dust, her Sunday shoes, the

41

library book she had lost last week, and a spelling paper — but no Rosemary.

She looked under the dresser and in the closet. There just wasn't any other place to look. Her door was safely closed, and had been all night, so Rosemary had to be somewhere in the bedroom.

Or did she? Zib suddenly remembered the wide crack under the door. In the days when Ruth and Karen had been better friends with her, they'd had a secret society one summer. They had often slipped folded notes, and even small packages, back and forth. But the space was scarcely wide enough for plump little Rosemary to squeeze through.

Zib searched the room again. She picked up her library book this time and dusted it off thoughtfully, putting it on the dresser where she would be sure to see it and remember to take it to school. She looked in the closet again, and hung up her red jumper which she had knocked on the floor. She picked up her sneakers and shook them, though she knew it was no use. She might as well start searching through the rest of the house.

Just as she'd expected, the bathroom door was locked. If she didn't get up before Ruth and Karen, they always got there first and made her wait for hours. She'd never have a chance now until they went down to breakfast. She shook the doorknob anyway, and pounded with her free hand.

"Who is it?" yelled Karen, turning off the shower for a minute.

"It's me," Zib shouted. "I want to look in there for something I've lost."

"Well, you'll have to wait. I'm all wet. Tell me what it is, and I'll look for it."

"No, I can't tell you. I've got to come in myself and see."

"If you won't tell me, you can't come in."

"Karen, please let me in! It's awfully important."

But the water was running again, and Karen wouldn't listen. Just then the door to the bedroom across the hall opened. Ruth dashed out in her pink striped pajamas, with her hair still up in bobbie pins.

"Hey, it's me. Let me in, Karen," she commanded, and flipped three times on the door with her fingernails. That was their secret signal this week.

The door opened and shut, and the bolt slipped into place while Zib was arguing.

"If you can let *her* in, why can't you let me in too? I've been waiting longer. And I've got to find my — my thing!" She tapped on the door with her fingernail as Ruth had done.

Ruth opened it and thrust something out at her. "Here's your old comic. You left it under the radiator."

"That's not what I'm looking for," Zib hollered. "Let me in and I'll tell you."

But the door was shut tightly against her.

"Go away!" Ruth yelled. "There's no room for three in here!"

Then Zib could hear the two of them laughing and chattering together. "That's the way it is," she thought. "Big sisters always cut you out."

"Breakfast is nearly ready, girls. Your mother says to hurry up!" their father called from downstairs.

"Be right down!" Zib called back. But she just had to find Rosemary first. She might as well be looking through her sisters' bedroom while they were showering.

Guiltily, she opened their door. They would skin her alive if they caught her in here without being invited. Their room was nearly twice as big as hers, because there were two of them to share it. It was much more interesting too, if you really liked their sort of stuff. It smelled of lipstick and bath powder and nylons. On their bed was a heap of clothes they'd pulled out of their closet while they were trying to decide what to wear to school. They did that every morning — tried on all their sweaters and skirts and scarves, and then usually ended up by trading with each other.

Zib looked hurriedly under their bed and dresser, and the slipper chair in the corner. She was on her hands and knees hunting through their shoes in the closet when Karen caught her.

"Well, for lop's sake! What are you doing?"

Zib scrambled guiltily to her feet. "I'm just looking for my —"

"Here's your old brush, if that's what you're hunting for. It was on the window sill at the end of the hall. Honestly, Zib, why don't you keep track of your things?"

"There wasn't anything else of mine — in the bathroom — was there?" Zib asked hopefully.

"Sure there was," Karen told her. "Your tooth-brush, your bath towel, and probably a washcloth. Now scram! I want to get dressed."

Zib took her hairbrush and went out into the small square hall, where she stood at the top of the stairway looking down. It was terribly steep. She had a sudden vision of Rosemary tumbling head over heels until she lay still and dead at the bottom. Or maybe she had just managed to climb down a step or two and was now hiding, shivering in a corner.

Zib flipped the light switch at the head of the stairs and peered down, but the old-fashioned light bulb was high in the ceiling and only made deep shadows on the steps. So she walked down slowly, feeling carefully with the toes of her shoes into each corner.

"Hey, you can have the bathroom now," Ruth called from the top of the stairs. But Zib didn't hear her. She went ahead, sliding her feet along the worn brown carpet to make sure she didn't miss Rosemary.

She looked carefully through the hall closet under the stairs. It was filled with galoshes, tennis rackets, and ice skates. It would have been a wonderful place for a little rat to hide.

Zib felt carefully in all the overcoat pockets. She wasn't sure how high Rosemary could climb, but at least she could scratch her way over the edge of the shoebox. If she was ever found again, Zib would build her a new wire cage with a hinged door, so she'd never get lost. If she was ever found — but she just had to be somewhere!

"Zibby!" said her mother, coming out of the dining room. "Whatever are you doing? Didn't you hear your father call you girls to breakfast? Why, you're not even dressed!"

"I'm just going to, Mom," Zib answered. "But I have to find something first."

"What is it?" And then without waiting for an answer, Mom went on, "You get right upstairs and put your clothes on. Don't stop for a shower. And tell those other two girls their eggs are getting cold. You're all going to be late for school."

"O.K., Mom." There was no use arguing.

She started for the stairs, but just as soon as her mother went back toward the kitchen, she scooted into the living room.

It was chilly and dark in here this time of the morning, but she didn't dare turn on a light. She started at one end of the room and methodically turned over every chair and cushion. She wiped her fingers under the two radiators, but there was nothing there but a bit of dust that her mother had missed in cleaning.

She felt along the edges of the couch cushions, and felt a nickel and two pennies. And she looked behind the television set and the old unused radio that stood in the corner.

She crawled on her knees beside the upright piano and wriggled her fingers along the edge of the rug. "Here, Rosemary! Come, Rosemary!" She clucked her tongue against her teeth, but there was no answer.

The next place to look was her parents' room. Zib opened the door cautiously, but it was empty. The weak early-morning sun was just coming through the smoky windows. Zib barely had time for a quick look around — under the bed, in the closet, and behind the chest. She could hear Mom out in the hall calling impatiently up the stairs. And then she heard Karen and Ruth come rushing down.

"Where can she be? I sent her up there ten minutes ago to get dressed!" Mom was saying.

"She's probably gone back to bed," Karen answered. "Do you want me to go up and roll her out?"

"No, you come in and eat your breakfast. You'll

all have to buy your lunches today. There isn't time to make sandwiches. I don't know why you girls can't take your baths at night. It makes such a rush in the mornings."

Zib heard them all go back into the dining room and shut the door. Mom was still scolding. Zib took one more look around and then ran upstairs. She would have to finish her searching at lunch. There was still the dining room and the kitchen. And the cellar. But poor little Rosemary surely wouldn't be way down in the cellar. She would have to slip out the kitchen door to the back porch and down those rickety old cellar stairs. And it was so cold down there. Zib shivered at the thought. "But I'll look, anyway. I'll look everywhere. I've just got to find her!"

Murder Mystery

— 5 —

ALL THE MORNING AT SCHOOL, Zib had a hard time keeping her mind on her work. She had a heavy feeling in her stomach, as if she had eaten too much breakfast too fast, but she knew it was because she was worried about Rosemary. She was afraid if she didn't start feeling better, she was going to have to ask Miss Barnes to let her go home.

She missed five words on the midweek spelling test; and when it came time for them to put arithmetic problems on the blackboard, she just sat, though usually her hand was the one waving most frantically.

Zib sat miserably watching the clock above the board. Someone must have stuck the hands down with bubble gum, the way they dragged. It never — it just never would be twelve o'clock.

The bell finally rang, and she was free to hurry home and start searching again. As she opened the front door, she reached hopefully into the mailbox. There was nothing for her, as usual — only one fat letter for Mom.

Only the two of them were home for lunch on school days, so they always had sandwiches or soup on the kitchen counter.

Mom had been baking pies for the P.T.A., and from the scraps of dough left over she had made a jelly tart for Zib's dessert.

Her mother cleared one end of the counter for their bowls, then sat down to open her envelope. "What a perfect surprise! It's a letter from Great-aunt Delia."

Great-aunt Delia was an old relative on Mom's side of the family. The old lady lived in Massachusetts, and all five of the Pauleys had been to visit her once — but that had been when Zib was a baby.

She had far more important things on her mind now. All the time she was eating, her eyes were roving around the kitchen trying to figure out where Rosemary might be hiding.

"Finish up your soup, dear," her mother said absently. And then, "Oh my gracious!"

"What's the matter?" Zib said, startled.

"It's poor old Aunt Delia. Her brother, Great-uncle Charlie, just died, and she's been left all alone."

"That's too bad," Zib said politely. But she was thinking, "If I were a lost rat, where would I be?"

She asked to be excused because there was something she had to do in the dining room. Her mother started to pick up the dishes, and Zib carefully closed the swinging door so she could search without being disturbed.

This was much harder than looking in the other rooms, because the dining room was so crowded. Besides the table, the buffet, the china closet, and all the chairs, there was the old red studio couch that they used to have in the living room before they had got the new set last year. Mom had decided that the old couch was too good to throw away and might serve as a spare bed when they had company.

Zib searched as well as she could without moving furniture, because to do that was nearly impossible.

She climbed on a chair and peered on top of the china closet, though she knew it was no use. Rosemary surely couldn't climb that high!

Well, she might as well start looking in the kitchen. Her mother was just taking another pie out of the oven. Zib bent down and began going through the cupboards.

"What are you looking for?"

"Just my — my social studies book. I think I left it in here somewhere."

It wasn't a very good fib. The way Zib said it she knew it sounded as though she were asking a question. She always wobbled her voice when she fibbed, and so people always knew.

"Your social studies book? In with the pots and pans?" her mother said. "Now don't tell me you're *that* absent-minded!"

Zib was poking hastily under the refrigerator with the broom.

"Now look, Zibby, what's the matter? You've been acting very strange ever since you got up this morning. It's not your schoolbook. You can't fool me. What have you really lost?"

Zib sat miserably back on her haunches. "It's Rosemary! She got out of her box last night, and I can't find her anywhere."

"Your rat? Didn't you promise to keep her up-stairs in your room?"

"Yes, I know I did, Mom. But she must have squeezed out under the door somehow."

"Have you looked everywhere upstairs? In your sisters' room? And the bathroom?"

"I've looked everywhere, all over the house. Es-pecially the bathroom! There's not a trace of her. I'm afraid somebody must have flushed her down!" Now she really began to cry.

Mom put an arm around her. "Don't be silly, Zibby," she said gently. "The creature's got to be somewhere in the house. Have you tried the cel-lar?"

"That was the very next place I was going to look," said Zib, wiping away her tears.

Her mother turned off the oven. "Well, I'll go down with you. It will be quicker if two of us are looking."

"Oh, thanks, thanks, Mom!" Zib sprang to her mother's side, thinking Mom was really a good sport about hunting for Rosemary, especially when you considered Mom didn't particularly like rats.

They spent the rest of the noon hour in the cel-lar, and came up with sooty hands and faces. But it was no use. Rosemary seemed to have vanished completely. Zib felt she couldn't bear the loss; nothing could take her mind off Rosemary.

That night, after the supper dishes were done and Zib's sisters had gone upstairs to do their homework, she lay on the floor watching a TV show. It was one she couldn't take her eyes away from, and yet every once in a while she'd think of Rosemary — the pretty, shy little ways she had, the trusting look her tiny eyes had for Zib. What if some cat, or some boys with a BB gun . . . ?

The show was a murder mystery, and things were moving along tensely and quietly. Any minute now there might be terrific excitement.

Above her, in the big chair, Daddy sat reading his newspaper, and now he too was watching, over the top of the paper.

Mom came in and sat down to watch too. "My goodness!" she said, "this is more than I can —"

Suddenly there was a terrible scream.

Zib thought for a moment it had something to do with the program, and then she realized it came from upstairs.

She stumbled to her feet and dashed out to the hall, but Mom and Daddy were there before her.

"What's happened up there?" he asked. "Are you hurt?"

Karen came to the head of the stairs, hopping on one foot and crying that something dreadful was in her slipper.

"I just put my foot in and it bit . . ." she wept, holding up her big toe.

Ruth coming behind her yelled, "That rat of Zib's!"

"Rosemary!" Zib yelped, ducking under her father's arm and scooting up the stairs. "Where is she now? Did you hurt her?"

"Did *I* hurt her? Look at what she did to my big toe!" Karen said indignantly.

Zib didn't wait to look at Karen's toe. She darted into her sisters' bedroom.

"What did you do with her? Where did she go? Is she still in your slipper?"

"No, she's not still in my slipper. I dumped her out, and she ran down the hall somewhere!" Karen said angrily. "What shall I do about my toe, Mother?"

Both parents examined it closely.

"The skin is barely broken, Karen," said her father. "Why don't you wash it off and dab it with some iodine?"

Zib, meanwhile, began searching the upstairs

bedrooms frantically. "Rosemary! Come, Rosemary, come, come!"

Then she went to look in the bathroom. Karen was standing on one foot, with the other one in the washbasin, trying to rinse her toe.

"Move over just a sec, Karen," Zib begged. "I think she's under this radiator."

"I don't care where she is!" Karen cried. "And stop shoving me!"

"You'd better let her find her rat," their father said mildly, "or you'll probably find it again yourself in your slipper in the morning."

Karen moved over then, so Zib could look under the radiator. And there was poor Rosemary, trembling in the corner. The bits of lint on her whiskers were dancing, she was so frightened.

Zib clucked her tongue at her softly. "Come on out, baby. It's all right now. That old Karen won't kick you any more."

"Ha!" said Karen. "If she thinks I kicked her, just wait until the next time!"

"There won't be any next time," Zib fired back. "I'm not going to let her get lost again. I'll build a cage for her." And she started for the stairs with Rosemary cuddled in her hands.

"Wait, Zib," Daddy said. "Maybe I'd better come

and help you. Let's go down to the cellar and see what we can rig up for a cage."

They found some pieces of chicken wire and a large square tin can that was quite clean. Daddy cut two sides out of the can and soldered chicken wire in place over the openings. It was not a very fancy cage, but it was secure. The only way in and out was through the round lid at the end, which would have to be pried up and pounded down again to close it.

"This will work fine, Daddy," Zib said. "She'll never be able to get out unless I want her to. What's the matter, Rosie, don't you like it?" For Rosemary was scurrying back and forth excitedly, sniffling and whimpering.

"Oh, she needs something to make her nest out of," Zib explained. "The cage is so big and bare it frightens her. Here, Rosie, you wait a minute and I'll get you some shredded paper and some food for your pantry."

As soon as Rosemary had her nest arranged comfortably and her food stacked in a neat heap beside it, she settled down contentedly, curled up, and went to sleep.

"Thanks for helping me, Daddy. We won't have a bit of trouble with her from now on!"

Petticoat and Parachute

— 6 —

FOR A WEEK AFTERWARD, all was peaceful. Rosemary lived quietly in her cage by Zib's bed, and the rest of the Pauley family nearly forgot the pet was in the house.

Zib borrowed Karen's best taffeta petticoat to wear to Janey's birthday party. The petticoat was very very full, with six or seven layers of nylon ruffles on the bottom. Karen had worn it only twice.

Zib never would have thought of asking to borrow it, but their mother mentioned how nice it would look under Zib's red velveteen jumper. And since Janey was Zib's best friend, it was important to wear something very special to her birthday party. Karen sighed and gave in. It was really generous of her.

She said Zib could borrow it if she would be very careful and not go spilling any ice cream on it. Zib asked how on earth does anybody spill ice cream on a petticoat. Besides, she didn't spill food any more, ever!

Of course it was too long for her, but since it only came to her waist, it could be tucked up easily under the elastic band.

Zib truly intended to return the petticoat immediately after the party, but she came home late. Janey had taken all of them to the movies and to the drugstore afterward for sundaes. Zib got home so late and tired she just tumbled into bed and didn't bother to hang up her jumper or the beautiful taffeta petticoat.

Both garments lay across the foot of her bed all night, and in the morning she saw to her horror that Rosemary had been busy. The petticoat must have dropped across the cage, which was beside the bed, and by working patiently Rosemary had managed to pull part of it through the chicken wire. She had chewed several large holes in the beautiful nylon ruffles!

"Rosemary!" Zib scolded. "What made you do such an awful thing? Now what am I going to tell Karen?"

"Tell me what?"

That was Karen standing in the door and looking curious. Then she saw the sad petticoat in Zib's hand, and she shrieked.

She shrieked so long and so loud that Ruth came running. Their father bolted in from the bathroom with his razor still in his hand.

Their mother came panting up the stairs, holding the pancake flipper. "What on earth happened? Karen, stop crying and tell me!"

Karen showed her the ruined petticoat, and Ruth said, "It's that dreadful animal. Mother, she's just got to get rid of it!"

"No!" Zib said. "It wasn't her fault. Really, it wasn't. I shouldn't have let the petticoat fall across the cage. She thought it was the same old rag I had given her to play with."

"Old rag!" Karen cried, more furious than ever.

"That's about all it is now," said Ruth, shaking her head sadly.

Their father started back to the bathroom.

"You might as well give the rat the rest of it, Zib," he advised offhand. "It will make her a very

sumptuous nest!" He was never fond of enormous petticoats. Made his daughters look like nail kegs, he claimed.

"This isn't a joke, Father," Karen said stiffly. "You seem to find it highly amusing when that animal of Zib's bites me or tears up my clothes."

"Of course I don't think it's funny, Karen. But it's such a magnificent relief, after I hear your desperate cry for help, to hasten in here and find merely that you've been nipped on the toe or that the trimmings on that outlandish tent of yours have been chewed! So I find myself inclined to levity."

"Whatever that means, Father. I think you are getting quite off the subject," Ruth said. "What we need to discuss is how Zib and that rodent of hers are to be punished."

"Elizabeth," Mother began, "I'm afraid this means —"

"No, please, Mother," Zib interrupted. "I'll pay for the petticoat. Honest, I will. Here, I'll get it out of my piggy bank!"

She opened the top drawer of her dresser and took out the fat little Mexican pig covered with the pink roses. After some shaking, a quarter and three dimes and two pennies fell out.

"Ha!" said Karen. "Thirty-five, forty-five, fifty-five, fifty-seven cents. That's just enough to buy me a new petticoat! Do you know what that one cost me? Four ninety-eight! Now where are you going to get that much money?"

"I'll take some out of my bank account," Zib said. "I've got nearly twenty dollars in there."

Ruth glanced at Father. "You said we weren't to touch the money in the bank, except in case of extreme emergency."

"That's right," he replied. "But, Zibby, I guess we could say this is a case of extreme emergency. I'll meet you down at the bank at noon today and help you withdraw five dollars to buy Karen a new petticoat."

And so the matter was settled. Karen grumbled that the new petticoat wasn't nearly as pretty as the other one. Ruth said something should be done about having rodents in people's houses, and Father said Zib was to promise to keep Rosemary's cage well under the bed, where there would be no chance of her chewing any curtains, bedspreads, or clothes.

After the Christmas holidays, Ruth and Karen

had an evening party for some of the high school crowd. Zib was allowed to help take the caps off the pop bottles and fill the plates of nuts and cookies, but other than that she was to keep strictly out of the way, preferably in the kitchen.

Most of the party was in the living room, where the rug was rolled up and there was a record player. It sounded noisy and like fun to Zib, but she didn't stick her head in. Her parents had gone out to dinner and a show, to get away from the confusion.

Zib, alone in the kitchen, opened a fresh box of cookies and piled them neatly on a plate.

"Hi there! How's Rosemary?"

Zib looked up to see Trek standing in the swinging door. "Oh, she's grown so much you'd never know her. Do you want to see her?"

"Of course I do. Dancing's all right for the other guys, but all I do is stumble over my big feet."

Zib took a quick look in the hall to see if Karen or Ruth was near.

"I'll go upstairs and get her. Wait right here and I'll be down in a minute."

Trek was in the dining room when she came back with Rosemary perched on her shoulder. He was passing the plate of cookies to three other boys sitting ill at ease on the studio couch.

"These are some of my pals who aren't much for dancing either," Trek said. "Ralph Jones, Steve Knight, and Nick Glass. This is Ruth and Karen's sister, Zib, and her hooded rat, Rosemary."

"How do you do?" said all the boys politely.

Trek held out his fingers to Rosemary. She sniffed them, and then turned back to Zib and squeaked something in her ear.

"What did she say?" Ralph asked.

"She says she doesn't know Trek any more," Zib replied. "He must have washed his hands."

The boys laughed at that, and Steve asked, "Is that the way Rosemary recognizes friends or enemies, by their smell?"

"Sure," Trek answered. "I'll bet she can pick Zib right out of a crowd. Let's make a ring around her on the floor."

Everybody spread out in a circle, and Trek set Rosemary carefully in the center. She lifted her little nose and sniffed, swinging her head back and forth anxiously. Then she caught Zib's scent, and turned and waddled straight toward her. She stood on her hind legs and tried to climb up Zib's slacks.

"Well, I'll be darned," Ralph said. "What else can she do?"

"Oh, she can ride in a little cart," Zib said.

"How is she on parachute jumping?" Nick asked. "Here, let's try her!" He snatched up a large orange scarf that one of the girls had laid on the buffet and began tying it around Rosemary's middle.

"Hey, that will never work," Trek said. "Give it to me, and I'll show you how to make a real parachute."

He and Zib went into the kitchen and got some long drinking straws, a paper cup, and some string. He tied the straws to the corners of the scarf and fastened their other ends to the paper cup.

"There now, in you go, Miss Rosemary, into the cup."

"Where will we drop her from?" Nick asked.

"I'm the tallest. Let me get on top of the table," Steve suggested.

"No, that won't be high enough," Trek said. "The chute wouldn't have enough time to fill out. Let's try the stairway."

They all went out into the hall. Trek climbed up to the top of the stairs and leaned over the railing.

"You won't let her get hurt?" Zib asked, but she was as eager as the rest of them.

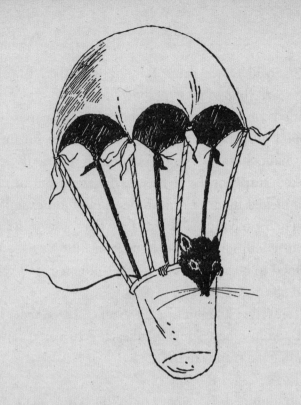

"Put plenty of pillows on the floor below," Trek answered.

Ralph slipped into the living room for cushions and returned with two more boys who wanted to see what was going on.

"We're going to have a parachute jump," Zib said. "You're just in time to see the famous Madame Rosemary make her initial leap!"

"Are you ready below?" Trek said.

"All ready, sir," said Steve. "Let her come!"

Swoosh! Down came Rosemary, with the beautiful scarf billowing out above her. And plop! She landed on the couch cushions. The paper cup tipped over and she scrambled out, then sat up on her haunches and groomed herself hurriedly. She looked suspiciously at the scarf spread out around her, picked up a bit of it in her paws, and examined it. Then, looking as if satisfied that it was still in good condition, she tossed it aside, gave what seemed to be a little bow to her audience, and waddled off toward Zib.

"Let's try it again!" said Nick. "Let's time her and see just how long it takes her to come down. Who's got a stop watch?"

"I have," said Ralph.

Zib dumped Rosemary into the cup again and carried it up to Trek for another jump.

"Ready! Get on your mark! Get set!" And just as Ralph said "Go!" Ruth's head came poking over his shoulder.

"What's everybody doing?" she asked.

The parachute swished down in front of her face, and Rosemary tumbled out into the pillows.

"Drat it!" Ralph grumbled. "You jiggled my arm and I missed count. Now we'll have to do it again!"

"Do what?" demanded Karen behind Ruth. "What on earth is going on here?"

"Hi!" said Steve. "Come join the party."

"The party is supposed to be in the living room, where the music is," Karen said furiously.

"Oh, this is a lot more fun," Nick said. "At this very moment you have the great good fortune to witness another big parachute jump by the Incomparable, the Fearless, the Magnificent Madame Rosemary! Is the timer ready?"

"Ready!" said Ralph.

"All ready up here," said Trek. "Hand me up the Madame, Zib."

But Zib saw the look in Ruth's eye.

"No, sorry," Zib said, "but we'll have to cancel all other performances. Madame Rosemary is exhausted. I must return her to her quarters."

She ducked up the stairs with the little performer clutched to her chest, and the groans of protest from Rosemary's fans ringing in her ears.

The party broke up soon after that. A little later, leaning over the banister, Zib heard her sisters reporting to Daddy and Mom as soon as they came in the front door.

"And she had all the boys clustered around her and that miserable little rat," Ruth said.

"Well," Daddy chuckled, "it seems as if Rosemary is a gal of unsuspected charm if she can so bewitch all the males. Especially considering she hadn't even been invited to the party."

"Invited!" screamed Karen. "Of course she wasn't invited. Neither of them was. Zib promised she'd stay out in the kitchen and help with refreshments."

"And as for that rat," Ruth added, "it was understood around here that it wasn't to be allowed out of its cage."

"And they used Marilyn Randall's scarf, and all the cushions from the living room!" said Karen.

"We didn't hurt a thing," Zib couldn't resist putting in, leaning farther over the banister. "Trek and Ralph and Nick said they didn't know when they'd had so much fun at a party. I heard them tell you that when they went home."

"They were just being polite," Karen said.

"And *we* didn't have any fun. Not a bit. And it was *our* party," Ruth wailed.

"Elizabeth!" Mom looked up the stairway at her. "What were you doing with that rat in the dining room? You promised —"

"But Trek asked especially to see her. And I

didn't think you'd want me to take him upstairs to my bedroom when I hadn't made up my bed."

Mom put her foot on a stair and said, "You mean to tell me your bed was unmade when we had all those guests in the house? Elizabeth Pauley, you march right into your room and make it now!"

Zib scurried back into her room. It was crazy to be making a bed just when it was time to be crawling into it. But she certainly wasn't going to argue when Mom had her mind safely off Rosemary.

Downstairs the talking got louder. Zib could hear Ruth saying angrily, "Mother, you let that child get away with murder!"

"You're surely not going to let her keep that horrible animal!" Karen added.

"Daddy, you've got to do something!" Ruth said. "All of the girls here this evening were just petrified while that rat was running around loose."

"But," Daddy laughed, "how could the rat have been running loose, when she was so busy as an entertainer?"

Zib heard the living room door slam shut, and there was silence at last.

She made her bed very carefully, smoothly folding down the sheet, then slipped inside.

Exiles

— 7 —

Z<small>IB WAS VERY CAREFUL</small> for a long time after that. She only let Rosemary out of her tin-can cage for a few minutes late at night. After everyone was asleep, she tiptoed downstairs to get bits of lettuce and bread out of the kitchen for her.

Ruth and Karen complained that they could hear the rat rustling the papers of her nest and chewing, and that the noise kept them awake.

It was true that Rosemary was noisiest at night, but Zib thought it was cozy to lie in the dark and hear her bustling about, cleaning and rearranging her little tin house.

No one seriously grumbled about Rosemary for several weeks, and Zib was beginning to hope that at last the family was going to tolerate her pet.

"Maybe now I can keep you forever!" she told Rosemary.

One Friday afternoon Zib came home from school to find the house all upset. Her mother was taking down curtains and rolling up rugs. It certainly wasn't housecleaning time. That usually came during spring vacation, just before Easter.

Zib stood in the front door watching, and wishing she had gone over to help Trek after school.

Her mother caught sight of her, so now it was too late to disappear.

"Oh Zibby, I'm so glad you're home. We'll go right upstairs and see about your room."

"I'm going to make my bed," Zib said rushing for the stairs. "I meant to do it at noon!"

"Wait, I'm coming with you, dear. I want to help you while we talk about it."

This wasn't at all like Mother, finding time to help with bedmaking, and right in the middle of housecleaning, too.

"We're going to have to change things around a little, Zibby dear." Mother was standing in the door, puffing from hurrying up the stairs. "I don't know what we can do about those curtains of yours. They're so shabby."

Zib looked at them critically. The curtains had been hanging there for almost as long as she could remember. Once they had been a gay pink, but now they were faded and limp. But she didn't really mind.

"And the dresser. My goodness, look how marred it is! Maybe your father will have time to sand it down and give it a new coat of paint."

"Plaid this time, Mother, please. It'll make everything look so bright. I saw a chest in a magazine done just like that. You just paste on wallpaper."

"Plaid!" Mother threw her hands up in horror. "Great-aunt Delia wouldn't care for anything like that, I'm sure. I think a nice soft rose —"

"What's Great-aunt Delia got to do with my dresser?"

Mother stopped short in her examination of the chest. "Why, you know I told you last week that Aunt Delia is coming to stay with us. You mailed the letter I wrote to her saying that we would love to have her."

Zib couldn't remember having heard one thing about it. Plans were always being made around this house, and talked over with Ruth and Karen, without her.

"How long is she going to stay?"

"I really don't know. Since her brother, poor Uncle Charlie, died last fall, Great-aunt Delia has been terribly lonesome. She finally sold the house they had always lived in, and then she wrote to ask if she could come and visit us."

"Why doesn't she go stay with some of the other relatives?"

"Now, Zibby! That certainly doesn't sound very hospitable. None of my cousins has as much room. They all live in apartments."

"Will she have to sleep with me?"

"Well, no, dear. That's what I want to talk to you about. There never would be room for two of you in that single bed. Besides, I'm sure Great-aunt Delia would like to have a room of her own. So I thought maybe it would be fun for you to sleep downstairs for a change."

"In with you and Daddy?"

"No, in the dining room. You could use the old studio couch. And I'll clear out a drawer in the buffet for you to store your clothes. Your dresses you can hang in the hall closet."

Zib thought this all over carefully, and then she

said, "I think she had better go to an old ladies home."

"Eliz-a-beth Pauley! I'm ashamed of you! Great-aunt Delia belongs to us. She was very dear to me when I was a little girl. I stayed with her a whole summer once when my mother was sick. And she was just wonderful to me. Now we're just about the only family she has left since Uncle Charlie is gone. Besides, old ladies homes are dreadfully crowded, and sometimes they're lonely, too. How would you feel if you were old and nobody wanted you around?"

Zib chewed her lips. "O.K., Mom," she said at last. "I guess it'll be all right. It'll be a change anyway, sleeping downstairs. Do you want me to start moving my stuff right now?" She reached under the bed for Rosemary.

"There's no real hurry, dear. Great-aunt Delia won't be here for a week or so. That will give you plenty of time to get everything settled and find a new home for your rat."

Zib plopped back on the bed, thunderstruck. "Find a new home for Rosemary? I can't! Why do I have to?"

"Aunt Delia would be terrified of a rat, Zibby.

Most old ladies can't bear things like that. Can't you understand?"

"But she wouldn't have to *see* Rosemary. I'll keep her safely down in the dining room. She'll never know I have her!"

"No, no, dear. Remember we all still have to *eat* in the dining room."

"I'll keep her in the living room then, behind the radio."

"Zibby, there's just no place for her," Mom said coaxingly. "You know that."

Zib got up and headed for the door. "There's no place for me either, then!" She turned and ran downstairs and out the front door. It wasn't until she got to the end of the street that she realized she was still carrying Rosemary's tin-can cage clutched tightly under her arm.

Zib was glad she had Rosemary with her, because the way she felt right then, neither of them was ever going back. She kept walking as fast as she could until she passed the cemetery east of town. There was an old crumbling wall along the upper edge of it. Zib set the cage carefully on a flat stone, and then boosted herself up beside it.

She pried the lid off with a stick and turned Rosemary out to explore. The little rat ran eagerly over the rough stones, raising her head to sniff the cool March air, and stopping now and then to chew on a slip of grass.

All was quiet and peaceful, Zib swinging her feet against the old wall and watching Rosemary play. Zib began to feel better inside. Still, it wasn't fair, she thought; but that's the way it was. You just got things all worked out and running smoothly, and then the grownups had to get some other idea and change everything.

The sun was getting low across the valley. Zib wished she had brought along a sweater. Rosemary came close to her and tried to snuggle under a fold of her skirt.

"Are you cold, Rosie? I guess we might as well go back home. Come on, you can ride inside." Zib tucked her pet down inside her blouse, then shivered and giggled to feel the damp little paws against her bare skin.

The Value of a Great-aunt

— 8 —

I<small>T WAS NEARLY DARK</small> when Zib turned into the driveway at home. Her father was carrying an armload of storm windows around to the back of the house.

"Hi!" he said when he saw her. "Missed you at supper. Where have you been?"

She liked to think he might have been just a little worried about her. After all, she had very nearly run away. But she said carelessly, "Oh, we went for a walk."

"We?"

She pulled Rosemary out of her shirt. "Yes — we, Dad. We went up to the old cemetery."

"Oh! You and it. Well, I think Mother saved you some supper. We had corn chowder — as we always do when we're housecleaning. Say, give me a hand with the door, Zib, will you?"

She opened the door of the back porch and helped him inside with his load.

He stored the windows under the back stairs and picked up a load of screens. "I don't think we can get these on tonight, but at least we can get the dust washed off them with the hose."

"Let me help you, Dad," she said. "I'm not hungry — not very."

She picked up the two screens that were left and followed him out.

"I've got to fix that bottom step one of these days," he said cheerfully. "You know, Zib, it's certainly good that Mother got me started on these windows a month early this year. Otherwise I'd keep putting off changing them until July, the way I always do. That's one good thing about your Aunt Delia's coming."

"She's not my aunt," Zib said bitterly. "She belongs to Mother."

"That makes her your aunt too. Your great-great aunt. She's your grandmother's aunt."

"She must be awfully old! Both my grandmas are dead."

"That's right, and the way I figure it a great-great aunt is worth a great-grandmother any day. And that makes her pretty important."

Zib was impressed. "People must get awfully tired of living so long. She must be about ready to die too."

"Oh, I don't think so," Dad said. "She's probably not much more than seventy-five or so. She was the youngest in a large family. Some of her brothers and sisters were eighteen or twenty years older than she. They're all dead, now that Great-uncle Charlie's gone, and that makes her pretty lonely."

"Well, I don't mind if she wants to come and stay with us," Zib said. "But I don't see why she has to be such a sissy about rats."

Dad propped the screens against the garage and then picked up the hose. "Turn on the water, Zib, please."

She turned the faucet, and he had to talk louder so she could hear him above the spray.

"You know, back where I grew up, on a farm in Iowa, rats were terrible pests. They ate grain and destroyed chicken eggs and even fruit. I used to shoot them with my .22 when I was about your size. If anybody had told me he wanted a rat for a pet, I'd have thought he was crazy."

"I know, Dad, but those were *wild* rats. Rosemary is different. She's a special laboratory strain. Trek says hooded rats are a mutation of *Rattus norvegicus,* which —"

"To lots of people, Zib, a rat is a rat, and it's pretty hard to think of them any other way. Especially when you're kind of middle-aged, like me, and set in your ways."

"But you like Rosemary, you know you do, Daddy."

"As rats go, she's good-looking, well-mannered and probably generous-hearted, but she's still a rat. I defended her loyally when your mother and sisters were all for throwing her out, and I'm glad you've had the experience of having her for a pet. But I must admit I wouldn't enjoy eating or sleeping with her. So you can imagine how Great-aunt Delia would feel, having to give up her cozy, quiet little house in Massachusetts and come here to live with our noisy family, to find we expect her to live with rodents!"

Zib didn't like that word, but she wanted to sound reasonable. "We at least can give Great-aunt Delia a chance to get acquainted with Rosie. She might even like her. You can't tell."

"I can tell, Zib. I've lived with old ladies before. They like to knit and crochet, and gossip a little, and have a light supper, and go to bed early. But they don't like dirty hands at the table, noise or confusion at any time. And they are afraid of rats and mice. You'll have to find a new home for Rosemary. That's all there is to it."

There was no use arguing with her father. Even when he said, "Let's talk it over," he usually had his mind already made up. And after he'd joked and talked all around, the answer was still the same.

That night, after Zib was in bed, Karen and Ruth came in to talk. They seemed really sorry about Rosemary.

Zib tried to glower at them suspiciously from her pillow. They never had tried to be friends with her and Rosemary before.

"Look," said Ruth. "I know where I can get you a little fluffy kitten. It's just darling. Part Angora, the girl who has it said."

"No thanks," Zib said, closing her eyes and hoping they would leave her alone.

They finally did. Then Zib got up, shut her door.

and got Rosemary out of her cage so they could play together on the bed.

It was late before Zib went to sleep. She kept thinking how Rosemary was still shuffling and rustling about happily, not even knowing that she was going to be sent away.

Zib saw Trek the next afternoon while he was out delivering his papers. She told him that she had to find a new home for Rosemary. "Would you mind taking her back? I'd rather you had her than anybody I know."

"Wish I could, Zib, but old Mamie has just brought forth another litter, and I'm having a hard time finding homes for them. Mom said absolutely no more animals until I unload those rats. Sorry."

"That's all right, Trek," Zib said. "One of the kids in my Scout troop would probably jump at the chance to have her."

But the Scouts weren't quite as eager as Zib had expected. Most of them shook their heads. Janey had a big tomcat; and Mrs. Thornton said she wouldn't mind having a pet rat, especially a well-trained, beautiful one like Rosemary, but she had two Scotties already, and they'd be death on a rat for certain. Nancy Soderberg said she'd ask her mother and call Zib after supper.

Zib listened all the while she was drying the dishes, praying that the telephone wouldn't ring. But it did, and it was Nancy saying joyfully that her mother would let her try taking care of Rosemary. She'd be over first thing in the morning for her.

Zib cleaned out the cage, scrubbed it, and gave Rosemary fresh bedding, letting her tears drip on the newspapers as she tore them into shreds.

Bobo's Double

— 9 —

A WIRE CAME FROM GREAT-AUNT DELIA that her train would be in at seven o'clock Thursday night. It was sooner than they had expected, but Zib's mother said everything had gone just beautifully. Zib was moved down to the dining room, and all her things stored snugly in the bottom drawer of the buffet. The extras that she had nearly outgrown, or rarely played with, were packed in cartons and taken down to the cellar.

Upstairs, the room was ready and waiting. The new curtains were hung at the windows, and the floor had been scrubbed and polished. The dresser had a fresh coat of enamel, and though the drawers were still a little sticky, they would be dry in a few hours.

Zib went up to her room for the last time, after school, just to see if she had forgotten anything. It looked like the room of a stranger. There was even a new smell about it. The bed looked different with her mother's rose chenille spread, which was really too big and hung nearly to the floor. But it was a great improvement over Zib's old faded flowered one.

She lifted the spread and looked under the bed. Without the familiar little cage, the floor looked bare and lonely. Rosemary had been at Nancy Soderberg's for a whole day and a night.

Zib had not planned on going to the station with the rest of the family. "I've got to go over to Nancy's and tell her something," she told her mother.

Really, she just needed to hold Rosemary for a little while. She didn't see how she was going to bear not seeing her any more.

"Now, Zibby, of course you're going with us," her mother said. "What would Aunt Delia think if you didn't come and meet her? She might think that you really don't want her to stay with us after all!"

Zib got in the car quietly. There wasn't any use arguing with anyone these days.

The train was more than half an hour late. After all the rush, hurrying through supper and leaving the dishes stacked in the sink, they all had to wait and wait. They stood outside by the fence squinting down the track. It was very boring, and after a bit Zib asked if she could go inside and see what time it was.

"Don't see why I had to come!" she muttered to herself for the fifteenth time. "Darned old Aunt Delia anyway!" It was eight twenty-five, she noticed. She could have gone over to Soderberg's and still have been here in plenty of time.

She picked up a comic from the magazine rack and was deep in an adventure of Little Lulu when she heard her father shout behind her.

"Hey there, Zibby! So that's where you've been. Aunt Delia's here!"

Zib turned around. Her family were all coming toward her, clustered around a little old lady dressed in a gray coat. Karen and Ruth each had a suitcase. Mother was trying to take a mesh shopping bag away from the old lady, who was hanging on to it stubbornly.

"You missed all the excitement of seeing the train come in," Karen said. "You and those old comics!"

Zib put the comic back on the rack guiltily. Mother put an arm around her, saying, "This is Zibby, Aunt Delia. I guess she was only a baby when you saw her last."

"Hello!" the old lady said, looking level into Zib's eyes.

Somehow Zib had expected her to be much taller. She had quick dark eyes that stood out in her wrinkled brown face. She had a broad snub nose and odd, wing-shaped black eyebrows. There was a black hearing-aid button in her ear, and a wire running down inside her coat. Close up she didn't look like an old lady at all. She reminded Zib of someone she had seen before.

"Well, you've changed a bit since we last met, Zibby," Aunt Delia said. "I believe you were wearing a pink bunting then and yelling your head off."

Zib ducked her head, embarrassed.

Her mother said, "Well, aren't you even going to give Great-aunt Delia a kiss?"

"Hi!" Zib said loudly and reached out her hand.

Aunt Delia set down her shopping bag and took Zib's hand firmly. She put her other arm around Zib's shoulders and gave a tight squeeze. Zib tried to pull away, but found that she couldn't. She had a queer feeling that this had happened to her before.

Aunt Delia brushed her cheek just for an instant against Zib's, and it was warm and dry.

Then Zib knew what it made her think of. Of course! It was the day, months ago, when she had gotten Rosemary from Trek. The squeeze Aunt Delia had given her, why even her face — the black eyebrows and the pug nose and the slash of a mouth — all made her look exactly like Trek's pet snake Bobo!

She started to laugh, but the laugh broke off in her throat and there was a cold feeling in her stomach. Bobo had been the first threat to Rosemary's life, and now it was Aunt Delia who was the cause of her being sent away.

"What's the matter with you?" Ruth asked curiously.

"Nothing," Zib said shortly. "Here, do you want me to help you with that suitcase?"

"It's not heavy," Karen said.

Zib slipped her hand through the handle and helped carry it anyway. Her eyes were stinging with tears, but she wasn't going to brush them away, for then everyone would notice.

When they got near home, they saw there was a car parked in front of the house.

"I wonder who that can be," Mother said, frowning. "It's late for visitors."

Dad swung past and turned into the driveway.

Zib opened the car door and jumped out. She had seen Nancy Soderberg sitting on the porch steps with the familiar cage on her lap.

"Hi!" Zib said. "Did you have to bring her back?"

"I'm sorry, Zibby. Really I am, but Mom said —"

"Sh!" Zib shoved Nancy behind her into the shadows of the porch.

Aunt Delia and Mother were climbing out of the car and coming across the grass. Mother was saying that she knew how tired poor Aunt Delia must be, and as soon as she had some toast and tea, she must go right up to bed. They were so busy talking, neither of them saw Zib or Nancy.

Karen and Ruth came behind, lugging the suitcases, and paid them no attention either.

Dad was pulling a heavy footlocker out of the trunk of the car. He bumped it across the grass and stopped at the foot of the porch steps.

"Just a minute, Daddy," Zib called out to him. "Do you want me to help you with that?"

"Here, I'll help you too, Mr. Pauley," Nancy said, setting down the cage.

"Oh. Hi there! I didn't see you, Nancy. Thanks, but this is too heavy for you girls."

"Of course it isn't," Zib said stoutly, getting hold of one end.

With the girls pushing on the bottom and Zib's father pulling on the top, they got the locker up the front steps and into the front hall.

"We'll just leave it here, and I'll go ask Mother and Aunt Delia where they want it," he said, and disappeared into the dining room.

"I've really got to go now," Nancy said. "Daddy's waiting for me in the car. Wish I could've kept Rosemary, but she bit my little brother. And Mom's afraid she might give him rabies."

"Rabies!" said Zib angrily. "She couldn't possibly have rabies. She's never been around any other animal who could have given it to her. And she never bit anyone else in her life." Then she remembered about Karen's big toe and the slipper. "Well, she hardly ever bit anyone else," she added.

"Oh, well anyway . . ." Nancy drew her breath fast. "I've really got to go! See you tomorrow, Zib." She ran down the path to her car.

Zib waited until she was sure nobody was in the

front part of the house before she walked over and
picked up Rosemary's cage. She peered in anxiously.

Rosemary was pacing about nervously, but she
looked unharmed.

That night, after everyone was in bed, Zib stole
out to the porch and brought Rosemary in. She put
the cage on the floor by the studio couch, and then
snuggled down under the blankets and listened to
the familiar sound of Rosemary tidying her house.
It was wonderful to have her home again, even if it
was going to be only for a little while.

Forest of Geranium Trees

— 10 —

EARLY THE NEXT MORNING, Zib put Rosemary's cage on the front porch and covered it with her red jacket.

"Where did you sleep, Zibby?" the pert little old lady asked at breakfast. "I have a feeling that it's your room I've usurped, isn't it?"

"Oh no," Mrs. Pauley said quickly. "Zibby has been wanting for ages to sleep downstairs. We've put her here on the studio couch."

"Here, in the dining room?" Aunt Delia said, startled.

"She doesn't mind. It's as much fun as camping out," her mother insisted. "Isn't it, Zibby?"

"What?" Zib muttered. She'd only been half listening. "Oh, I don't mind. It makes a nice change, and I don't have to be across the hall from those dopes!" Before Karen and Ruth could jump at her, Zib added quickly, "Excuse me, please. I've got to get ready for school." And she dashed upstairs to comb her hair.

There wasn't time to hunt for a hiding place for Rosemary. The only thing to do was to take her to school. Maybe Miss Barnes wouldn't mind, especially as soon as she realized the rat was her namesake.

As Zib walked along carrying the cage, she could think of lots of reasons why Rosemary would be welcome in the fifth grade. Actually, rats were very educational. Now take arithmetic. A nice big cage could be planned for the classroom. There would be measurements, and Miss Barnes could make a good problem out of how much lumber and nails and chicken wire it would take to build it. How much would it cost, say, if chicken wire cost — Zib wasn't sure just how much chicken wire did cost, but Miss Barnes would appoint a committee . . .

Miss Barnes looked a little uneasy when she saw Rosemary. "Well," she said, "I've never been quite this close to a rat before. Will she bite?"

"No," Zib promised. "Pet her. She loves to be petted."

Miss Barnes timidly stroked Rosemary's back with one slender finger tipped with rosy polish. "Why, she's quite an interesting animal, isn't she?" she said in pleased surprise. "And she's so clean. Somehow I always thought of rats as being quite unpleasant creatures."

"Oh, she's never unpleasant," Janey put in helpfully. "Rosemary's always cheerful and amiable."

"Rosemary?" Miss Barnes asked a little breathlessly.

"Yes, I named her after you." Zib tried to smile. "When she was a little baby, she sort of reminded me of you. Of course now she's big, she doesn't look so much like — "

"Especially her teeth!" said Peter Brock, who sat across the aisle from Zib. "Her teeth are a lot longer than Miss Barnes's."

The fifth-graders roared with laughter. Comparing the rat's sharp fangs with their teacher's even white teeth!

"Oh, I think she has pretty nice teeth for a rat," Miss Barnes said. "A rat dentist would probably say she had wonderful teeth."

"They're buckteeth!" Peter scoffed.

"If my dentist saw them, he'd put braces on them quick as that!" Diane Smith said. "Mine weren't nearly that bad, and look what he did to me!" She opened her mouth wide to show everybody her shiny wires.

"The rat isn't supposed to be pretty like you, Diane," Miss Barnes said. "Her teeth don't have to be straight and even. As a matter of fact, hers work better if they are long and extend over her lower jaw."

"Buckteeth, like I said," Peter insisted.

"Maybe so," Zib said hotly, "but she can gnaw things with them a lot better than you can with yours, I bet."

"She can gnaw what kind of things?" Peter asked.

"Oh, hard bread and apples and grain."

"Well, I'm pretty good with apples and bread, but I'll let her have all the grain she wants," Peter grumbled. "I tried chewing some raw wheat once, and I didn't like it at all!"

"What makes her teeth so yellowish?" Diane asked. "Is that because she can't brush them?"

"She doesn't need to brush them," Zib said. "With all the hard things she eats, she keeps them clean.

They're a good clean yellow. That's just their nat-
ural color. I think all grown-up rats have yellow
teeth — like hers."

"My dog has yellow teeth," Peter said, "and
they're sure not dirty. He polishes them on the
bones he chews — like this." He chewed like a
dog. That started all the fifth-graders off on a noisy
acting out of tooth-polishing.

Miss Barnes finally had to say, "Shush, all of
you hound pups. Put your bones away and take
out your arithmetic books!"

"Miss Barnes," Zib said, still holding Rosemary.
"I have a wonderful idea how we can use Rosemary
for a problem in arithmetic."

She explained as quickly as she could, but when
she paused to catch her breath while telling about
getting up a committee, Miss Barnes held up her
hand.

"Let's leave that for another time," she suggested.
"Today you might write compositions on the subject of pet rats."

So after arithmetic the class wrote compositions
on whether they thought rats were useful or
harmful to humans. Janey wrote an essay on how
rats were helpful in laboratory experiments. She

had to go to the library to look up some of her information. So did Peter. He needed to find out how much damage rats did each year to farmers' crops. Zib wrote a story of how wonderful it was to own an interesting, lovable pet like Rosemary, and when Miss Barnes suggested the class vote on the best compositions to pin to the bulletin board, Zib's was one of the first to be chosen.

It was a very successful day, Zib thought as she picked up her books to go home.

Miss Barnes said, "Thanks for bringing your rat, Zib. My goodness, I never dreamed we could learn so much from having her here. Maybe she'll come again sometime."

"I'd be glad to leave her now for a few days, Miss Barnes," Zib said hopefully.

Miss Barnes picked up her red pencil and started to correct papers. "That's very generous of you, dear, but we aren't set up here to take care of pets. We enjoyed having her today, but I think it's best you take her home now."

Zib felt tears begin to sting her eyes. "That's just the trouble. I can't keep her at home." She started to get all choked up, and she couldn't speak for a minute. She was acting like a dreadful baby, but

Miss Barnes put down her pencil and came down the aisle to sit beside her.

Zib then felt she had to tell all about how hard she had tried to keep Rosemary out of everybody's way so her family would not complain.

"I tried to find another home for her. I've tried and tried. Nancy took her, but she had to bring her back because Rosemary bit her little brother. I'm sure he must have been teasing her, because she's the gentlest animal. Really, she is!"

"I know she's a very lovely rat. And very dear to you, Zib, but I don't see how we — "

"We could keep her cage on the window sill behind the geraniums," Janey said, coming up. She had been standing at the door waiting for Zib. "That way Rosemary wouldn't be any bother to anybody."

Zib looked at her gratefully, and her friend went on loyally, "She'd make a good pet for our whole class. We could take turns taking care of her, and we'd learn an awful lot!"

"Well," said their teacher, "I guess we can try it for a day or so. But it would be wise for us to keep this just our class secret. You can't be sure some other people in the school won't be disturbed if they know there s a rat here."

Zib and Janey understood. They rearranged the potted plants so there was room for the cage just behind them.

"It looks now just as if she were living out in a forest of geranium trees," Zib said happily. She felt as though an enormous weight had been lifted from her shoulders.

Wearing of the Green

— 11 —

THE NEXT DAY WAS ST. PATRICK'S DAY, and in the excitement of having Rosemary at school, Zib completely forgot to wear something green. By recess time her arms were so sore from having all the other kids pinch her and yell "Greenie on you!" she decided she'd ask Miss Barnes if she could stay inside and look through the supply cupboard for a piece of green crepe paper to make herself a hair ribbon.

"I'll straighten the shelves for you too, Miss Barnes."

"That's a wonderful suggestion, Zib. They certainly need it. Do you want anyone to help you?"

Zib looked around. Janey and Nancy were signaling to each other. She knew that meant they had a game of jacks planned for recess.

"No thanks, I can work faster alone."

The rest of the class filed out, and Zib started to straighten the shelves. She took Rosemary out of her cage and let her perch on her shoulder to watch.

Zib couldn't find a bit of green paper, not even any green construction paper. There was only some red and white left over from Valentine's Day, and stacks and stacks of blue-lined penmanship paper. At the back of the middle shelf were several tall bottles of ink. One of them was a bright green!

"Hey, Rosie, maybe we can think of some way to use this! I think green fingernails would be nice. I'll bet not a single soul in this whole school has green fingernails today. And you, Rosemary — you need something green too. I know! A lovely green tail. Then we'll really be celebrating!"

It took only a couple of minutes to paint the fingernails, using a bit of Kleenex for a brush, and less than a minute to paint the tail. There was still plenty of time and ink to do more, so Zib touched up Rosemary's whiskers with green tips. Then she quickly peeled off her shoes and socks and worked on her toenails.

"We might as well do this up with a bang, Rosie!"

She heard the kids coming down the hall, back from recess. There were splotches of ink on the floor, and her toes weren't dry yet, but she yanked on her socks and left her shoes untied. She dampened a rag and wiped up the spots on the floor as best she could, hustled Rosemary back in her cage, and stuffed the ink and stacks of paper back into the cupboard. It wasn't a very good job of straightening the shelves, but maybe Miss Barnes would let her stay after school and finish.

Soon after the class got started again, a girl came in from the principal's office with a message from Miss Rathmore. It was weighing and measuring day, and they were to go right down to the nurse's office.

The fourth grade had filed in ahead. So while the fifth grade was waiting in the hall, Miss Barnes suggested they could be taking off their shoes. Zib saw with horror that her white socks were spotted green. Golly, but her mother was going to be mad when she saw them!

Miss Rathmore was coming down the hall just then, urging everyone to keep straight in line and *please* stop whispering and giggling.

She stopped beside Zib and looked down at her feet. "What happened to you?" she asked coldly.

"I guess I spilled some — some green — ink."

"On your socks?" Miss Rathmore said incredulously. "It looks as though it's soaking through."

Zib didn't say anything.

"Well, take them off!" Miss Rathmore said. "Let's see what you've done!"

Zib leaned down with a sigh and pulled off her socks. Not only her nails, but her toes too were now bright green.

"Well, I've never seen anything quite like that!" Miss Rathmore said. All the fifth-graders crowded around to see too.

"Get back in line, boys and girls." That was Miss Barnes coming up from the end of the line. "Is anything wrong, Miss Rathmore?"

The principal just pointed to Zib's feet.

Miss Barnes bit her lip. Zib had a feeling Miss Barnes was trying hard not to smile. "I guess it's St. Patrick's Day, Miss Rathmore."

"Well, I know it's St. Patrick's Day, Miss Barnes. But on St. Patrick's Day we wear a green dress or a little green bow in our hair. There's certainly no need to paint ourselves all over with green ink. Just look at her fingernails!"

Miss Barnes looked, but did not smile. She had to agree that Elizabeth had behaved quite disgracefully.

Miss Rathmore said Elizabeth had better come sit in her office while it was decided what further measures should be taken.

Zib trudged into the office and sat on the straight-backed chair by Miss Rathmore's desk.

It was unusually quiet out in the hall. Miss Rathmore was probably helping with the weighing and measuring.

Zib stayed there in the office until the noon bell rang and all the children trooped out for lunch. But nobody came to tell her she could go home. She thought she'd been forgotten. Then it was twelve thirty, then twenty to one and quarter to. Finally Miss Rathmore came and stood in the door looking at her. "Well — ? Why did you do it?"

"I had forgotten what day it was, and — and I needed something green to wear, and I couldn't find any green paper."

"So you took it upon yourself to take some of the school's ink and decorate yourself."

"It seemed like a good idea when I did it," Zib said humbly.

"But it doesn't seem so now?"

"Not very," Zib admitted.

Miss Rathmore thought a minute of what best should be done with this awful child. "Well," she said finally, "I think you had best go straight home and scrub all that ink off your hands and feet. And believe me it won't be easy. Unfortunately, you chose the permanent variety. Check back into the office here when you are all scrubbed clean. I'm afraid your mother is going to be most unhappy when she sees your pretty white socks."

Miss Rathmore was right. It wasn't easy to scrub off the green ink. It seemed to have soaked right into her finger and toe bones. She scrubbed and scrubbed until the skin was raw.

Her mother shook her head in disgust when she saw Zib, and threw up her hands when she saw the socks. "I don't think it will *ever* come off. It will probably have to wear off. And we might as well throw the socks away. Zib, what makes you do things like this?"

Aunt Delia heard the fuss and came out of her room to see what was going on. "Maybe I can help, Zib. Lemon juice will sometimes take out ink stains. I'll go down to the kitchen and fix you some."

The lemon juice made Zib's sore fingers and toes smart, but the stains gradually faded until they could scarcely be seen.

Later, Aunt Delia dyed the socks a bright green to match the spots. So the socks were saved.

Next day when Zib returned from lunch, Janey and Nancy, looking horrified, met her in the hall.

"Golly, Zib, guess what's happened!" Nancy said.

"Not Rosemary! Nothing has happened to Rosemary!" Zib said in panic.

"She's disappeared," Janey said.

"We don't know how she got out — " Nancy was saying.

But Zib didn't wait to hear more. She raced down the hall and up the stairs to the fifth-grade room.

Miss Barnes and all the class were hunting; some had gone down the hall, wandering in and out of the other classrooms.

"We're supposed to act as though we're not searching for anything, because of our class secret, you know," Diane said. "But we're going to try to cover the whole school."

"It's just like being detectives," Peter whispered as he tiptoed by.

Miss Barnes was busy looking in her desk drawers. "I don't see how she could possibly be in here, but we're not going to overlook a single place. We've just got to locate her!"

"We'll find her, don't worry, Zibby," Janey said comfortingly.

"I think she'll try to come back to her cage," Zib said. "She always does that at home when I turn her loose in my room."

"When I *used* to turn her loose in my room," Zib thought. "I don't even have a room of my own any more; and even if we find Rosemary, I probably won't ever be able to keep her at home!" But this wasn't doing any good, standing around grieving.

"Is it all right if I go downstairs to the auditorium to hunt?" Zib asked Miss Barnes.

"A good idea. On your way, you and Jane might carry those folding chairs back that we borrowed last week for the mothers' meeting."

Janey and Zib each picked up a chair and started down the steps. The tardy bell had rung, and the halls were deserted except for an occasional stealthy fifth-grader trying to look as though his business was anything but looking for a lost rat.

"You know," Janey said, "I'm afraid it was all my fault, Zib. I might have left the lid up when I looked at her during recess today to see if any of that green ink had rubbed off her tail. I guess I didn't shut the lid tight, and she might have gotten out when we were at lunch."

"You have to whack it down hard, Janey. That's all right. She couldn't get very far by this time."

Janey set down her chair and held the heavy auditorium door open so Zib could go in. They unfolded the chairs and arranged them at the end of the row.

"Where shall we start looking?" Zib whispered. There was something about the bigness and bareness of the room that made her want to whisper.

Just then they heard an ear-splitting shriek. There was a rush of feet in the hall and excited voices.

Janey looked at Zib, and Zib said, "That sounds like — "

They started for the door. There was a crowd of children in the hall in front of Miss Rathmore's office, and several teachers were all talking at once.

"Let me through! Let me get by!" Zib began to push her way into the office.

Miss Rathmore was standing on her desk with her skirts held high above her knees. Rosemary was nowhere to be seen.

"It's over there!" Miss Rathmore was exclaiming. "It's a horrible creature with a green tail!"

Zib crawled on her hands and knees behind the desk, making the clucking sound with her tongue. "Come on, Rosie! Nobody's going to hurt you!"

She could see Rosemary now, standing on her hind legs sniffling bewilderedly.

"Come on, baby!"

Rosemary waddled toward her, and Zib scooped her up.

"Elizabeth," gasped Miss Rathmore. "Elizabeth Pauley, could that animal belong to you?"

"Yes."

"Well, get her out, get her out of here!"

Zib looked at poor Miss Rathmore still standing high on the desk, trying to smooth her rumpled skirts. She felt embarrassed, and sorry for her being so terrified by a little rat.

Miss Barnes motioned to the fifth grade.

"Back to your rooms now, everyone," she said in her even voice. "Zib, you'd better take your rat straight home."

"Can't I just go back up to our room and get her cage?"

Miss Barnes shook her head. "Don't stop for anything." She opened the big front door for Zib.

"Hurry right home and then come right back to school."

Only Aunt Delia was at home. She called down the stairs when she heard Zibby come in. "Your mother has gone shopping. Is anything wrong?"

"No," Zib said. "My teacher just sent me home for something."

She went straight to the dining room and sat down on the couch and looked all around the room for a safe place to hide Rosemary.

Of course! The top of the china cupboard. It was tall, and carved rather like a castle tower. All around the top edge was a sort of wooden wall about four inches high, just like a parapet. It was a good place to store small things that weren't used very often, because they weren't visible unless you stood on a chair.

Zib climbed up to look. There was the old Indian bowl with a chip out of it, piled high with some gilded pine cones from Christmas before last.

"Here, Rosemary, you have a nap in here until I get home from school. You always sleep all day anyway."

Zib moved some of the pine cones and tucked a piece of Kleenex in to make a soft nest. Her pet rooted among them suspiciously.

"Please, Rosie, you've just got to settle down! I'll bring your cage home just as soon as I can. And then we'll figure out what to do with you next. But please be good for now. Go right to sleep. Just until I get home!"

Obediently, Rosemary pulled the Kleenex over herself and snuggled down. She'd had enough excitement for a while.

A Date

— 12 —

ZIB EXPECTED TO BE CALLED IMMEDIATELY into Miss Rathmore's office for an explanation. But Miss Barnes told her that the principal had gone home with a bad case of nerves.

"I'm afraid you and I will have to face her together tomorrow," Miss Barnes said. "But at least there are two of us in trouble, and we can help each other."

Zib took the cage home at noon, but she had no chance to slip it into the house. Aunt Delia was sitting on the front porch knitting, and Mother was in the kitchen fixing lunch, so Zib left the cage in the garage.

After school, Aunt Delia was still on the porch rocking happily. "Hi there, Zib! Isn't it a wonderful day to be outdoors?"

"She's sitting there just like an old bull snake waiting to catch Rosie," Zib told herself.

"Is that you, Zibby?" her mother called from the kitchen. "I need you to do some errands for me."

The errands took nearly an hour. She had to take some bundles over to the church for their overseas box, and then buy some groceries. When she got back, it was time to set the table for supper.

Aunt Delia had moved into the dining room with her knitting. "It's getting cool outside," she explained. "Do you want me to help you, Zib?"

"No thanks, Aunt Delia," Zib said politely. Inside she was thinking, "The best way you could help would be to take yourself out of here so I can do something about poor Rosemary."

With the six chairs around the table, it was very crowded. One of the chairs had to be smack against the china cupboard. She set Aunt Delia's place there, so the old lady would be facing the other way, in case Rosemary poked her head over the edge.

But right now, all was quiet above. Rosemary was probably still asleep.

There was chicken pie for dinner. It was probably very good, but to Zib it tasted just like mush. All she could think was, "Hurry, hurry, all of you. Get through supper and go into the living room, so I can rescue Rosemary!"

"I'll clear the table," she offered, aloud.

"No, you won't!" Karen said. "It's your turn to wash."

"Oh, I'll wash too. I'll do it all myself. Then you can all go in and watch television together. I think there's — "

Up on the china cupboard was Rosemary with a front paw lifted, peering inquisitively over the edge.

"No! No! Rosemary, go back!" Zib made her mouth say without speaking aloud.

"What's the matter, Zibby?" her mother asked anxiously. "Did you get a chicken bone? And I was so careful — "

"Rosemary, please! Don't lean over the edge like that!" Zib prayed silently. "You'll fa-a-ll!"

"Zib!" said her mother again. "Do you have a bone caught in your throat?"

Zib pulled her eyes back to her plate. "No, I'm fine, thanks, Mother!" She took another bite of chicken pie. "Don't jump, Rosemary," she begged silently. "Whatever you do, *don't jump!*"

Rosemary didn't jump, and she certainly didn't fall. She made up her mind, and carefully and deliberately scrambled over the edge, then clambered straight down the side of the china cupboard so quickly and neatly that the family scarcely had time to turn their heads toward her.

Zib heard the scritch-scratch of her toenails on wood, then the soft plop of her landing on Aunt Delia's shoulder. Then a jump and she was on the table, eagerly approaching Aunt Delia's chicken pie.

"What on earth!" Dad exploded.

"Oh, for lop's sake!" said Karen, pretending to collapse.

"I thought Zib had given that awful creature away!" Ruth said, folding her arms tight and trying to look calm.

Mother just sat with her mouth sagging open, and shaking her head a little as if it were too horrible to believe.

But Aunt Delia raised her eyebrows a little and said, "Why, what a nice, pretty rat! And with a green tail! I believe he's hungry!"

All the family spoke at once, loud and angrily. Zib knew it was no use trying to explain until they got it all out.

Aunt Delia looked at her and winked. "Is he yours, Zib?"

Zib nodded. "But it's a *she*, Aunt Delia. Her name is Rosemary."

"Does she live up there on the china closet?"

"No, she has a cage out in the garage, but I just haven't had a chance to — "

"I'm sorry, Zib, but I can't hear you, everyone is talking so loudly." Aunt Delia tapped on her water glass with her fork.

Everybody immediately shushed.

"Now this isn't such a dreadful thing to have happen," Aunt Delia told them. "There's no need to scold Zib. If I'd been a rat left on a strange china closet all day with no dinner, and I smelled delicious chicken pie, I'd probably invite myself to dinner too."

"The rat had no business being on the china closet," Mother broke in. "Zib was to have found another home for it last week."

"I did, Mother. But Nancy had to bring Rosemary back because her mother wouldn't let her keep her."

"Rosemary?" Aunt Delia said. "She looks as though she'd celebrated St. Pat's Day right along with Zibby. You know, I have never before seen a rat with a green tail and whiskers! Makes her look most dashing."

"The kids at school — "

"What!" Dad said. "You took her to school? It must have caused a riot!"

"It just about did," Zib admitted, and she told them how the fifth-graders had hunted and hunted for Rosemary, and how funny Miss Rathmore had looked, perched on her chair with her skirts held high.

The family rocked with laughter. Zib could feel all their angry feelings melt away.

"But, you know, somehow I felt sorry for Miss Rathmore," Zib said, sobering. "She's such a big, tall lady and she was so scared. She's probably scared of lots of things, even though she scares other people."

"That could well be, Zibby," Dad said gently. "And then what happened?"

Zib told them the rest of the story. "I didn't mean to leave Rosie up on the china closet so long, but I was busy running errands all afternoon, or else there was always someone here in the dining room."

"That was me," said Aunt Delia. "Sitting underfoot here knitting. It isn't enough that I push Zib out of her own bedroom, but then I have to plant myself in her way so she can't attend to the needs of her own pet. Well, Zibby, we're going to change all that. If I'm going to be part of this family, either I'm going to sleep down here on the couch, or else we'll move it upstairs and you and I will room together, with Rosemary."

"Oh, but she can't keep that rat!" Mother said. "You couldn't have a rat in your bedroom, Aunt Delia!"

"Why not? I've always wanted a pet, but Brother Charlie never could stand animals in the house. I had to be satisfied with a barn cat. Now at last here's my chance!"

"But you couldn't sleep with her in your *room*, Aunt Delia," Ruth said. "She makes so much noise at night."

"She grits her teeth and rustles, and keeps us awake for hours," Karen added.

"Oh, that won't bother me a smidgen. I turn off my hearing aid every night anyway. The roof could fall in and I'd never hear a thing."

Aunt Delia picked up Rosemary and put her on her shoulder. "Well, we've got that all settled, Zib. Go get Rosemary's cage, and I'll fix her a dish of this chicken pie she was so interested in."

Zib and her aunt went out to the kitchen together, leaving the rest of the family just sitting around the table, staring at each other in wonder.

Zib stopped at the foot of the screened-porch steps and turned back to her aunt. "Things don't bother *you* very much, do they, Aunt Delia?"

"You mean like having rats drop from nowhere in the middle of my supper?"

"You know, Aunt Delia, you remind me of a friend of mine," she said suddenly.

"Oh, who is that, dear?"

"His name is Bobo. At first I didn't like him at all. I was scared of him, I guess. And I thought — well it's hard to explain, but I like him very much now. You'll have to meet him, and then you'll see what I mean."

"I'd like very much to meet him, Zib. Where does he live?"

"He lives with another friend of mine named Trek. You'll like him too. We'll go to see them tomorrow."

"It's a date!" Aunt Delia promised. And she held the kitchen door open wide so that Zib could see her way out to the garage for Rosemary's cage.